TIMELESS
TALES TO TELL
Esther Tucker

<u>Preface</u>

Throughout my life I have struggled with inner battles that I believed I needed to face on my own. I never wanted to burden anyone else with my troubles, especially when they seemed so insignificant. Everyone has problems and I didn't want others to think that I believed mine were worse than theirs. Eventually that mindset mostly subsided. I still try to avoid asking for help when I need it, but I no longer push people away when they see my hand barely above the water and try to save me from drowning.

I know that there are many people out there that still struggle in the ways I did. I know that it may be challenging to rely on anyone else for assistance for a multitude of reasons. Asking for help can sometimes be a harder task than working through your troubles on your own, and that's okay.

While writing these parables and poems, I realized that what I have been missing was never the support that I needed. I never needed a big light shining down on me, showing me where to go. I never asked for a clear cut path railroading me to where I needed to be. I was always right where I was intended to be. Many days it felt like I was drowning. I was lost on an unknown island, or stuck in a storm, or waiting for the skies to clear up so I could escape. Even though I had these feelings, I always had a way out.

We are surrounded by people who are willing to help. People who want nothing more than to see us succeed. Even when you can't see them, or they seem far away, or you don't want to bother them by asking, they're always there. I know it may seem like you have to fight your battles on your own, but just know that you always have an army right behind you, waiting to help you home.

I'm Not Lost

In my hands I hold a map.
It has all of my adventures
and all of the paths
I may choose to take.
The one for Joy
is marked in green.
It takes me through the forest,
on long hikes in the woods.
The one for Peace
is marked in blue.
It takes me to the ocean
towards the waves and the breeze.
The one for Hope
is marked in Gold.
It takes me forward
never winding back.
In my hands I hold a compass
always pointing towards You.
No matter what path I take,
I need the map
and the compass
to guide me safely home.

JOY

To my siblings, for always showing me I can find my own path, even though they are always there to guide me if I lose my way.

The Girl the Sea Stole

There was once a young girl named Joy. Joy found herself marooned on a desert island, alone and afraid. Her ship had sunk and she had drifted to this uncharted part of the world on scraps of debris. She had no hope and no direction. Despite all of this, Joy was determined to survive. The island she had washed up on was abundant in resources. It seemed like everything she needed to survive was within her reach. She had plenty of trees to make a shelter and to cultivate a fire. She had plenty of fruit to gather. There was an abundance of fish that remained in the shallow water, close enough that all she needed to do was reach out and grab one.

Up to this point, Joy's life had never been easy. She had fought for every job, saved for every bite, and worked for every day that she was able to get. Despite her troublesome past, Joy was not skeptical of this magical oasis. She believed that she had worked hard to earn this easy life. Every day on the island she would wake up and hear a little voice telling her how she had earned this new life. It told her that she deserved to feel joy and peace. This same little voice made her forget her old life.

Several years passed and Joy got used to life on the island. She had built a small tree house, made tools for hunting and foraging, and even sectioned off small pools of water to make catching fish easier. These years of simplicity were pure bliss to Joy, especially with the voice always there to remind her how much happier she was on the island than she was in her old life.

One day, Joy woke up and the voice was gone. It was not quieter or coming back later in the day. It was just... gone. And everything came back to her. Suddenly the peaceful island was too quiet. The solitude no longer felt safe. The freedom became too much. And all Joy felt was fear. Without the reassurance of the voice Joy had no direction. She realized that she was truly alone, and the island's perfection melted away.

Instead of giving up, Joy decided to search for the voice. First she did what many of us do when we lose something. She checked the last place she had it, or could remember having it. Joy had heard the voice for so long that before it disappeared, she had begun to tune it out. She knew she heard it at sunset, telling her that she was blessed to have seen such a sight. But when she checked the beach where she always said goodnight to the sun and the sky, the voice was still gone.

She checked her pools next. She was pretty sure she had thanked the voice for telling her how hard she had worked to earn her now easy meals. However, when she gazed into the water, all she saw was herself gazing back. She did not look like herself. She looked more tired. One of her eyebrows was up too high while the other remained down, leaving her confused. Thankfully a fish swam through her reflection, bringing her back from her daze.

After looking everywhere else she could think of, Joy decided to try to search the entire island at once.

She started the long hike to the top of the mountain the next day at sunrise. It was more difficult than she remembered. Normally the voice would be there, cheering her on, telling her there were only a few more steps. Without it, Joy felt weak and brittle. She never worried about failure or injury until the voice left.

Still, she continued on. If she could just get to the top of the mountain, she believed she could find the voice and be whole once more. The journey took longer than past travels. Time slowed as she moved onward and upward. It was several days before Joy made it to the summit of the mountain. Once she arrived, she looked around, searching aimlessly. She had failed her quest, or so she thought. As she looked out over the mountaintop, across the ocean of trees to the sea beyond, she was struck by the beauty of it all. This island, her island, was magnificent. She spotted birds she had once ignored, more colorful than the rainbows that peaked out from behind storm clouds. She found coves near the shore, glistening with shrouds of mystery and wonder. She saw how the treetops hugged the sky in a wonderful, imperfect horizon. And at the end of the day, as she gazed out over the island and watched the sun set behind the waves that had brought her to her new home, Joy finally, truly, thanked the voice. She thanked it for her hardships that she had endured to end up here. She thanked it for the trees, for the sky and for the island. She thanked it for leaving her, so she could truly view and appreciate all that she was given.

11

And in that moment, the voice returned to welcome her, saying He had missed her while she searched, but that He was glad she had finally found true joy.

Thank you for always being there when I need you, but for also giving me the space to grow into who I have become. Even when life seems like it's more challenging than before, I know that at the end of the day it is just as beautiful as it was when we were young and I always had you by my side, bringing me joy.

Peace

To my friends, who are always there supporting me, even when I can't see them.

<u>The Girl the Sea Tested</u>

There was once a young girl named Peace. Peace was often found out in the water, exploring the sea that reached the horizon. There were several days when she returned and was greeted by her friends and family, all commenting on how well she managed her ship. They all seemed impressed that she was able to keep it afloat and in good condition all on her own out at sea. Even though Peace sailed alone, she never felt that way. She always had clear skies that made navigation easy, and the waves always seemed to stop before crashing against her hull.

With the sea and the sky on her side, Peace knew she was never alone. She always had her compass, and that was enough to guide her. While it seemed like a lot to others, Peace always knew that no matter what happened, she would always be able to return home safely, with her ship in good condition and a smile across her face.

One morning Peace decided to venture out on her own again. The sun was just peeking over the horizon and the sky was lit red. Most sailors would have taken this as a warning, and Peace did. But she was stubborn and despite knowing that a red sunrise meant there were storms on the way, Peace trusted in her luck and set sail.

It was several hours before the first cloud was seen. It crept up from the west, as ominous as a shadow stalking its prey. Peace tied everything down just to be safe. She checked the hull for leaks before the storm hit and found none. Everything seemed to be in perfect condition, ready to weather the battle ahead. She went back up to the stern to make sure she was still on course and froze. Her compass, her guiding light and sign of luck, was not where she normally left it. An unmistakable feeling passed over Peace as the first drop of rain fell and met her cheek. Fear.

Now, at this point in Peace's life, she had sailed through many small storms. She knew she could handle the wind and the rain as long as her hull held strong. Even without her compass, she knew these waters well and was sure of herself. She was so confident in her abilities that she continued sailing straight on, into the storm.

Peace remained calm and composed as she steered through the growing waves. Her confidence did not waver for the first several hours, but there is only so much battering that any ship, and any man, can take before they begin to crack.

She was almost out of the storm when she felt her ship begin to drag in the water. It was no longer slicing through the waves, but instead it was holding onto them. She ran below decks to find the issue and was horrified. Her once pristine cabins were all flooded, taking on more water every second.

Peace did not hesitate. She immediately began to frantically work the pumps, trying to get the water out of the hull. She knew then that she would be stuck until the storm passed on its own. Above decks there was no kind sky. There was no gracious wind helping to guide her home. There was no way for her to anchor in order to hold her ship in place safely. As

Peace rode out the storm, the storm she knew she could have avoided, the storm she saw in the morning sky, Peace wept.

She cursed the sky for turning on her. She yelled at the sea for attacking her. And she screamed at herself for allowing the sky and the sea to do these things to her. As she wept, the water below decks continued to rise. It was up to her hips now, pressing against her sides. The water was not being pumped out as quickly as it was being pooled in. Even still, as the waves from inside the rocking ship beat at her sides, Peace felt something shift in her pocket. She moved her hand to catch it and realized with relief that it was her compass. Her way home and her good luck charm. It had never left her side, it was just out of her sight and away from where she had searched. Peace breathed an immediate sigh of salvation. Knowing that her compass had remained with her gave Peace a reason to continue onward. She gained her second wind and began pumping the water even faster.

Eventually, the storm passed. Peace was able to remove all of the water from below decks and find the areas that needed to be patched. She knew that she was still at the sea's mercy and that the water was still too deep to anchor, but with her compass once again in her hand, she trusted that she would be safe and find her way home.

By the time Peace returned above decks, soaked through and bruised from her hours of labor, the sun was setting and a beautiful red light hugged the sky. Peace smiled to herself and to her compass, knowing

that the next day would be clear skies and smooth
sailing for her return home.

Thank you for always talking me through my storms. Even when I think I'm taking on too much water, you always remind me to take it one wave at a time and eventually I'll make it out again and be at peace.

Hope

To my parents, who continue to guide me towards the lit path, even when I manage to fall astray.

The Girl the Sea Saved

There was once a young girl named Hope who was in love with a lighthouse. Or at least, that is what most people assumed. Every week at the same time, on the same day, Hope would get on a ship and make the long journey across the sea, just to see the beacon that the light-keeper cast. It was not a treacherous journey. There were no pirates littered among the waves or sea monsters infesting the depths below, waiting to strike. It was just a straight sail. There were never storm clouds on lighthouse day and the wind was always being caught in the sails, helping the journey go even faster. The sun always shone on lighthouse day, and the clouds were few and far between.

Every week, Hope always wore her favorite dress and her brightest smile to show the light-keeper. Every week she would get excited before the journey, happy to explore the lighthouse once again. She would traverse the steps, memorizing each corridor as she passed. She would make up stories about past visitors, imagining them as though they were much different than her. She would race to the top of the tower and lean on the railing, peering at the small ships and smaller people down below. And just like everyone else who visited, she would admire the light and listen in as the light-keeper told her and others about how it guided ships and people to safety.

Because of this, most people assumed that Hope was in love with the lighthouse. It was not unheard of, as many people devoted their lives to taking care of the lighthouse and leading others to its guiding light.

While it was not unheard of for someone to be in love with the beacon, it was still wrong in the case of Hope. You see, Hope was not in love with the lighthouse. Yes, she enjoyed her visits, but she never understood the people who worshiped and followed the lighthouse, nor did she care to understand.

What Hope truly loved was the light-keeper. He always showed Hope extra attention and allowed her to wander more than others because the light-keeper was actually Hope's father. Because he lived with the lighthouse, though, Hope could only visit him once a week. This made Lighthouse day Hope's favorite day.

As Hope grew, her home island moved farther away from the lighthouse. The seas seemed to become more stormy and the clouds blocked out most light. Hope, once accustomed to the smooth seas of her youth, feared sailing in these conditions. She told herself and the light-keeper that she would visit again once the sea was calm and the sky was clear to guide her. It never was. As soon as a ray of sunlight pierced the dark sky, it was blocked out and the torrential downpour began again.

Hope was not alone on her island and had little reason to want to leave. She worked most days, even the days she was in school. Through her work and her studies, she met many amazing people. These people made her forget the lighthouse and the light-keeper for many years.

There would be days where the sea would be calmer or the breeze would blow in the correct direction, calling her back to her childhood. On these days, Hope, who was much less young now, would look towards the lighthouse and wonder about the light-keeper. Still she never visited. She was much too busy with work and her studies now and failed to find the time. It was not until some of the visitors on the island began retelling the tales she had heard when she was young that Hope truly thought about returning.

Now, by this point, Hope had grown from a young girl into a young woman. She was intrigued by the stories the visitors told. She remembered the light-keeper telling them to her as she wandered around the lighthouse, but she could not figure out what they meant. Questions weighed her down and curiosity filled her mind. She needed the answers, and knew there was only one place to go to find them.

Hope knew where she needed to go, but she was still afraid of the darkness. She asked for advice from the visitors, who had quickly become her friends. They looked at her kindly and with love in their eyes. They told her there was nothing to fear and that the light from the lighthouse would guide her safely there. Still, she was fearful. She asked about the waves and how to avoid them. Once again, her friends reassured her and told her the seas would be calm for her journey. Still unconvinced, Hope asked about the storms. Her friends smiled and told her to trust that the joy she held would reflect in the clouds.

This last bit of advice confused Hope, but she decided she was ready to take the journey regardless. The night before her trip, she did everything she had done in her youth. She set out her favorite dress to show the light-keeper. She found a new copy of the old tales the light-keeper told, and she dreamed of clear skies. The next morning she awoke full of positivity and optimism that was reflected in the clouds, just as her friends had said.

She went to the ship that would take her to the island, already prepared for the journey ahead. As she boarded, she noticed that the waves seemed calmer. And as the ship launched, she noticed that the wind was at her back, aiding her travels. Once underway, Hope smiled. She smiled a full, ear to ear grin, and the sun illuminated her joy.

Just as the visitors had told her, it was smooth sailing to the lighthouse. She arrived on time, but remained at the port. Uncertainty crept its way into her mind.

What if the halls she had once memorized had changed?

What if the steps had fallen or the light-keeper had forgotten who she was?

As soon as she saw him, all of Hope's worries melted away. He walked to the pier to greet her and wrapped her in His warm embrace. He never asked her why she had stopped visiting. He never scolded her for not trying to see the path He lit for her. He simply held her, and led her back towards the light.

Thank you for always being there for me to
return to when I need you. Even when I
choose to live on my own, I know you're
always there behind me, giving me hope.

In Your Eyes

When the day looks bleak
and the sky is full of clouds,
I turn to you.
I see your joy.
I feel your warm embrace,
and know that I am safe.
When I fear I have lost
and I can not find my way,
I turn to you.
I see your peace.
I feel the love in your gaze,
and know that I am safe.
When I think I can not go on,
and that continuing will get me nowhere,
I turn to you.
I see your hope.
I feel your trust in your guiding hand,
and know that I am safe.
Even when I fail to see you
or to feel you close,
I know you are there,
watching over me,
keeping me protected
and I know that I am safe.

Life is full of ups and downs. It throws rocks and sticks at you, attacking you from all sides. The days when the sun turns off are often the worst, because you can no longer see where the attacks are coming from. On those days it can sometimes help if you just close your eyes. I know it's already dark, and it can be frightening to lose what little sight you have, but if you just close your eyes and focus on where you feel the attacks coming from instead of trying to see what's attacking you, you'll be able to avoid getting hit more than if you kept trying to dodge the shadows you think you see.

You don't have to travel to a desert island to find joy. You don't have to brave a storm and almost drown to find peace, and you certainly don't have to forget the happiness from your past to find hope. You are fully capable of getting through whatever comes your way. Even when the outlook seems dark and it looks like things won't get any better, just hold out a little longer, and wait for the sun to come up.

Acknowledgments

I could never have found these stories without the help of my family, both chosen for me and chosen by me. Each of these parables is a reminder that no matter what I face, I always have support. I have many days where I feel like I'm just trying to make it to tomorrow, hoping for it to be better, but writing these stories helped me realize that I don't have to wait for better days to come find me. I can go out and make the sun shine and help each day be brighter than the last.

It took me several years to understand that the world is going to reflect what you believe it will show you. Thanks to my friends and family I am finally able to see the world in a new light. A brighter light. Thanks to my siblings, I have found joy. True, unmistakable joy. Thanks to my friends I have found peace. A peace that allows me to keep moving forward. Thanks to my parents, I have found hope. Hope that tomorrow will always be better than today, and that yesterday was no worse than the days before.

About the Author

H.R. Penn is from a small town in Western Kentucky. She started writing poetry in high-school and continued throughout college. She struggled with depression and used writing as an outlet. She wrote these poems and parables one of the nights when she was feeling lower than usual and hoped they would help others who feel the same.

www.ingramcontent.com/pod-product-compliance
Lightning Source LLC
Chambersburg PA
CBHW061032100726
47911CB00006B/167